Larry's LATKES

by Jenna Waldman

illustrated by Ben Whitehouse

APPLES & HONEY PRESS

To all of my favorite taste testers,
and in memory of my own Grandma Gators.
—JW

Forever for Yvonne, Timmy, and the
Whitehouse family.
—BW

Apples & Honey Press
An Imprint of Behrman House Publishers
Millburn, New Jersey 07041

Text copyright © 2021 by Jenna Waldman
Illustrations copyright © 2021 by Ben Whitehouse
ISBN 978-1-68115-565-4

Library of Congress Cataloging-in-Publication Data
Names: Waldman, Jenna, author.   Whitehouse, Ben, illustrator.
Title: Larry's latkes   by Jenna Waldman ; illustrated by Ben Whitehouse.
Description: Millburn, New Jersey : Apples & Honey Press, an imprint of
Behrman House Publishers, [2021]   Summary: "Big Larry, an alligator
with a latke food truck, decides to celebrate Hanukkah with a new latke
recipe"-- Provided by publisher.
Identifiers: LCCN 2020035465   ISBN 9781681155654 (hardcover)
Subjects: CYAC: Stories in rhyme.   Latkes--Fiction.   Cooking--Fiction.
Food trucks--Fiction.   Hanukkah--Fiction.   Alligators--Fiction.
Jews--Fiction.
Classification: LCC PZ8.3.W145 Lar 2021   DDC [E]--dc23
LC record available at https: lccn.loc.gov 2020035465

The illustrations within were created using digital tools.

Design by Elynn Cohen
Edited by Alef Davis
Printed in China

1 3 5 7 9 8 6 4 2

1121/B1780/A6

Big Larry has a latke truck he brings out once a year.

The customers wait round the block when Hanukkah is near.

They chitter-chatter happily, a lively, laughing line,
then crunch up every crispy crumb—

For many years Big Larry flipped his pancakes with a mission.

His Granny Gator's recipe hangs high inside his truck.
It fills his heart with memories and always brings him luck.

His party starts at five o'clock, and he wants something new.

A special party recipe—
the same old spuds won't do!

The farmers market bustles as Big Larry checks each stall.
He twirls his tail of rugged scales and wants to try it all.

The rows of friendly farmers flaunt their produce:
"It's first-rate!"

He picks the perfect PEPPER,
TOMATILLOS for good measure,
a bursting bag of YELLOW PEARS
that shine like golden treasure.

He doesn't buy a single spud.

Big Larry lumbers to his truck with food to fry and try.

But PEACHES are a soggy mess, and TURNIPS are a flop.
A LEEK, a PEAR, some CAMEMBERT—make mushy-gushy glop!

He fries some KALE—"I will prevail!"—a QUINCE, a CUKE, a LIME,
some RAINBOW CHARD—

This won't be hard!

—he adds a pinch of THYME.

When claws turn pink and stain the sink, Big Larry starts to fret.
The farmers see him struggle—"Wait! You haven't tried these yet!"

His pancakes sizzle in the pan.
"Oy vey, these don't look right."

He dashes through the market on a gator-tater quest.

He scoops a massive armload,
and his friends haul all the rest.

His truck is busy, bouncing, as the joy inside him grows.
The splendid spuds have brought an end to all his latke woes!

"Potatoes mix with PEACHES, and potatoes mix with BEET."

"An APRICOT won't hit the spot? With TATERS it's complete!"

It's five o'clock, and round the block
are CHAG SAMEACH! wishes
as applesauce and sour cream
make trails around the dishes.

30TH ANNUAL
HANUKKAH
PARTY!

Larry's LATK

Big Larry licks his gator lips and eats a PERFECT bite.

Menu

A NOTE TO FAMILIES

It was a miracle that Big Larry's latkes were ready in time for his party—but Hanukkah is all about miracles! The story of Hanukkah tells us how, long ago, a tiny flask of oil lasted for eight days when it should have only lasted for one. The oil kept the lamp lit as the Jewish people repaired the Temple. Today, we fry latkes in oil to remind ourselves of this miraculous event. Larry and his friends found a creative way to honor this Hanukkah tradition by cooking new latke recipes. Now it's your turn! Grab your apron, stomp your gator feet to the kitchen, and start cooking!

Big Larry's Rainbow Latkes with Fresh Rainbow Salsa

A note to families: Kids can help with mixing and measuring, but make sure that an adult handles all the peeling, chopping, frying, and latke-flipping.

makes about 12 latkes

Ingredients

2 medium yellow potatoes, peeled and shredded

1/2 large yellow onion, finely chopped

1/2 cup kale, thinly sliced

1 egg, lightly beaten

1/4 cup matzah meal or breadcrumbs

1/2 tsp. salt

1/2 large beet, shredded

1 yellow pear, peeled and chopped

olive oil for frying

1/4 cup tomatillo, chopped

1/2 cup bell pepper (red, orange, yellow), chopped

2 tbsp. chives, chopped

1 tbsp. lemon juice

optional: thinly sliced Camembert and sprigs of thyme for garnish

Directions

1. Mix potatoes and onion and place on cheesecloth or a tea towel. Squeeze out as much liquid as possible, then place mixture in a large bowl. Add kale, egg, matzah meal, and salt, and mix well.

2. Combine shredded beet and chopped pear in a separate bowl lined with a cloth, and squeeze gently to remove some of the liquid. Add the beet and pear to the potato-onion mixture.

3. Heat one inch of olive oil in a large frying pan. Form three-inch patties and place them in the pan three or four at a time. Fry each batch until both sides of each patty are golden, about three to four minutes on each side. Place on a paper towel to drain.

4. To make the rainbow salsa, combine the chopped tomatillo, bell pepper, and chives in a small bowl. Add lemon juice and mix well. Spoon the salsa beside the latkes.

5. Optional: Top the latkes with thinly sliced Camembert and sprigs of thyme.